THINK COOL THOUGHTS

by Elizabeth Perry
Illustrated by Linda Bronson

CLARION BOOKS · NEW YORK

Clarion Books
a Houghton Mifflin Company imprint
215 Park Avenue South, New York, NY 10003
Text copyright © 2005 by Elizabeth Perry
Illustrations copyright © 2005 by Linda Bronson

The illustrations were executed in acrylic and oil.
The text was set in 18-point Loire.

www.houghtonmifflinbooks.com

Printed in Singapore

Library of Congress Cataloging-in-Publication Data
Perry, Elizabeth, 1959–
Think cool thoughts / by Elizbeth Perry ; illustrated by Linda Bronson.
p.   cm.
Summary: On the hottest night of the hottest part of a very hot summer, Angel, her aunt, and
mother drag their mattress to the rooftop to sleep and hope for cooler weather.
ISBN 0-618-23493-4
[1. Heat—Fiction. 2. Summer—Fiction. 3. Rain and rainfall—Fiction. 4. Aunts—Fiction.]
I. Bronson, Linda, ill. II. Title.
PZ7.P4348Th   2005
[E]—dc22   2004014427

ISBN-13: 978-0-618-23493-6
ISBN-10: 0-618-23493-4

TWP   10   9   8   7   6   5   4   3   2   1

For Benjamin, Thomas, and Piper

—E. G. P.

To Charlie and Frannie

—L. B.

One summer, in the hottest part of the summer, came a day so hot after a week so hot after a month so hot that chocolate bars melted before you could eat them, and the pavement stuck to your sneakers.

When the nights came, they were even hotter than the days.

"Think cool thoughts," said Angel's mother. "Think of snowstorms and icicles. Think of the frozen wind blowing down from Canada, across fields and fields and fields of winter." She brushed the damp hair back from Angel's forehead. "Think of the coldest, deepest water in the ocean."

But the ocean was too big and winter was too far away. In the thickness of the night, Angel lay on top of her sheets and imagined ice cubes, small and close. She was good at counting, so she counted while they melted in her mind, smoothing the sticky wrinkles of the sheet beneath her. One . . . two . . . three . . . four . . . five . . . six . . . She tried to get up to a thousand. A thousand ice cubes melting might make magic. She wanted to believe in magic. Something—anything—to end the hotness.

"When I was your age—" said Aunt Lucy.

"You were seven?"

"I was seven and your mother was five and we had a summer like this one . . ." Aunt Lucy and Angel's mother were sitting in chairs by the kitchen window, talking about Aunt Lucy's hard times. It was difficult to imagine them any smaller than their own sizes, but Angel tried. She could think of them with their legs swinging, Aunt Lucy's bare toes just touching the floor, her own mother's feet swishing in the hot air. For just a moment, she felt as if she were looking at an old photograph, and then it faded in her mind.

"That was the summer after your
grandfather died," said Aunt Lucy, "and it got so hot
that we took our mattresses out on the roof."

"You slept outdoors?"

Aunt Lucy nodded.

Angel looked over at her mother.

"We'll have to see," she said slowly.

But her mother was smiling the smile that meant "yes" for special treats as
long as you didn't fuss about them, so Angel smiled back on the inside, and
didn't say anything more about it.

9

Later that afternoon,
they dragged her mother's old
mattress *lump bump bump* up all the
stairs, and the hottest air got even hotter,
because it mixed with the sweat on their faces and
the mattress dust and the stair carpet dust that they kicked
up with the lumping and bumping and bumping along. Angel
and her mother pushed and squeezed the mattress, and Aunt Lucy
tugged and pulled the mattress up and up and up the last stairway to the
roof. *Pop, flump*, at last. They pushed the mattress to the middle. *Whew!*
Angel sat down. Her mother let out a great breath and sat down beside
her. "We're just a little crazy—you know that?" said Aunt Lucy, and she
laughed and sat down, too.

Sitting between them on the mattress, Angel looked up. The sky was a different shape, and bigger than the usual blue rectangle between the buildings. The roof sky was round like the sky in the park, but even closer.

Angel hugged her sweaty knees, feeling the sticky mattress dirt dribbling down inside her elbows, while her mother and Aunt Lucy brought up sheets and pillows and chairs for later.

One . . . two . . . three . . . four . . . five . . . six . . . seven . . . melting ice cubes.

That night, after her bath, Angel got to sleep on the roof in her underwear.

Eight . . . nine . . . ten . . .

Slowly the round sky got dark and purple without letting go of any hotness.

Eleven ... twelve ...

The wrinkles of the sheet stuck to her and she stopped counting her ice cubes and pretended to be asleep.

The grownups were talking, but the words were
not important. Angel could hear the rhythm of a question
and an answer and a question and the beginning of another
long, long story about someone she didn't know. Her mother and
Aunt Lucy sat on the kitchen chairs and drank ice water. As she got
sleepier and sleepier, they became giant shadows against the sky.

In Angel's dreams that night, all the buildings in the city sat down on kitchen chairs to rest. They leaned together to talk in quiet voices about the stars in the sky and the little streets like threads below them. Angel was happy, and pigeons were dancing with ice cubes on every rooftop. She snuggled up in her sheet to watch.

When she tried to roll over, Angel bumped against a
giant bony shoulder. She tried to roll the other way and bumped
into a great big warm back. The sky was gray-lavender, the color of
dishwater, and not dark purple anymore. Only one star was left. Angel
wiggled over onto her stomach and lifted her head.

Straight across the street, the windows were so pink and so gold that she knew in her heart that ice cube magic must have changed the world while everyone slept. She had to believe in it, because every edge, every speck of every brick in that building was rosy and distinct.
A little breath of breeze lifted a blue curtain out of a kitchen window and let it drop back in again.

19

It was warm between her mother and Aunt Lucy, but not hot. *Not hot.* Angel was ready to shout, I AM NOT HOT! The air moving past her face was cool. So cool. Just brushing its coolness against her cheeks and eyelashes. She whispered, "I am not hot," in the tiniest voice she had.

"*Mmff,*" said the warm back.

"*Fffssshh,*" sighed the bony shoulder.

The breeze gusted, three pigeons flew past with their sudden disorganized flapping, and two fat raindrops landed— one on Angel's hand and one on her ear. Her mother woke up fast. Aunt Lucy woke up, too.

"Quick, Lucy," said Angel's mother. "If the mattress gets wet, it will be forever drying."

"Angel, darling, you take the sheet and pillows," said Aunt Lucy, stretching her back as she stood up, "and keep them off the ground."

They hustled the mattress inside and lumped it in a hurry down all the stairs. Angel followed, watching the grownups bent in all directions, squeezing the mattress back into the apartment. She felt like the Statue of Liberty, holding up the sheet and pillows as she stepped carefully after them.

Then they all went back up to the roof to get the kitchen chairs, to bring them in out of the wet.

"Don't stop me," said Aunt Lucy, and she sat right down on one of those kitchen chairs. "My goodness, oh, my goodness," she said. "After all that heat."

"Mmm," said Angel's mother, and she sat down, too. And they just let the rain wash out of the sky, right through their hair and into their faces, like wet statues in their summer nightgowns. They didn't move.

Angel looked up into the big round sky. She opened her mouth
wide and caught the rain in little splashing sips. She spread her fingers apart
and let the rain get in between them, wiggled her toes, and began to twirl and
dip and bop like the pigeons and the ice cubes in her dream.

27

Her mother and Aunt Lucy began to laugh at Angel dancing in her underwear. The sound was wetter and cooler than the water fountain in the park. They hadn't laughed like that in the whole month Aunt Lucy had been staying with them.

Angel kept on dancing and spinning as they laughed, around and around and around. And then somehow the dancing and laughter brought music along with it. She began to sing. The tune was the church tune, and the words were partly her own new words, which came from inside her:

> "I love this rain, how sweet the sound,
>   It falls on you and me
>   And on the roof and on the ground.
>   I'm cool, I'm wet, I'm free."

She sang it again, and Aunt Lucy began to sing the harmony. The rain kept coming down, her mother was still laughing and singing a little bit, too, and that was the exact moment the hottest part of that very hot summer began to end.

And from that cool dancing rainy morning on, even
when Angel decided she was really too big to believe in
magic, anytime it began to get hot at night, she counted
ice cubes. Just to help things along.

One . . .

Two . . .

Three . . .